Cottontip
Wins the Race

BY LINDA L. BURNEY

Illustrated by Angel Dela Pena

Print information available on the last page

Rev. date: 01/30/2016

To order additional copies of this book, contact:
Xlibris
1-888-795-4274
www.Xlibris.com
Orders@Xlibris.com

This book is dedicated to children of all ages
who find special grace in life whenever they
place another's needs above their own.

"Cottontip! Come here, Cottontip!"
Mother Rabbit called her little bunny.

Cottontip was playing in the grassy yard behind the cottage. He ran in and flopped down in a chair.

"Cottontip," said Mother Rabbit, "you must take these four pies to Mrs. Mole's house. They are for the fair tomorrow."

"But, Mother" Cottontip protested, "I must go to the field to practice for the big race tomorrow. I can't do both. Can I please take the pies later?"

"No, Dear," Mother Rabbit answered. "The big race is important, Cottontip, and it is also important for Mrs. Mole to have these pies for the fair tomorrow. Whenever you can, you must always do what is important to someone else, before you do what is important to you, my little bunny. When you make others happy, you will be happy too."

"Now put on these oven mitts to protect your hands, and get started;" said Mother Rabbit. "Remember, you can carry only one pie at a time. And, my little bunny, if you hurry, you can also practice for the big race."

Mother Rabbit's words sounded good to Cottontip, so after he put on the large green oven mitts, his mother carefully placed the first pie in his hands, and kissed him on the cheek. Cottontip walked slowly out of the door, then he scampered down the long trail to Mrs. Mole's house. He ran past the field where his friends were practicing for the big race. He ran past the trees where the birds were rehearsing cheerful songs. He ran past the pond where the ducks were practicing for the swimming contest. Everybody was getting ready for the fair tomorrow - everybody except him.

Cottontip ran faster. Mrs. Mole's house was a long distance away and he had to hurry and finish so he could practice too.

Mrs. Mole was waiting on the porch and opened the door for Cottontip.

"Hello, Cottontip." she said, "Please place the pie on the cooling table that is next to the stove."

Cottontip carefully set the hot pie on the cooling table, whizzed past Mrs. Mole, and jumped off the porch. He was on his way home to get another hot carrot pie.

"I'll be right back!" he yelled, as he took off down the winding path. All the friends of Green Patch Cove stopped to watch as Cottontip ran past them with another steaming hot pie, then another one, and then the fourth pie.

They wondered why he was doing that instead of practicing for the big race tomorrow. Each time Cottontip passed them he ran even faster than before.

At last, all the carrot pies were finally on Mrs. Mole's cooling table.

Cottontip was finally finished, but now he was exhausted. He lay down on a stool next to the cooling table to rest.

"You have done a good job, Cottontip," Mrs. Mole clapped her paws and said, "Now off you go. You must get home before it gets too dark. Your mother will be waiting for you to get home safely. Thank you so much, Cottontip!" Mrs. Mole was so happy and Cottontip felt good inside.

"You're welcome, Mrs. Mole," he said, "I'm glad I could help." Then he waved good-bye to Mrs. Mole and ran home faster than ever.

Only now, it was dark outside, all of his friends had left the field, and he didn't even get a chance to practice for the big race. Cottontip was very disappointed.

The next morning, Mother Rabbit was eager to go to the fair. They arrived early to get a good seat.

"Come now, Cottontip," she said, "after the birds sing their cheerful song, the big race will begin." Cottontip was still very sad.

"I didn't get a chance to practice yesterday, Mother. I'm not ready for the big race today," Cottontip said. Mother Rabbit stroked his face. She was not worried at all.

"I think you got all the practice you need, Cottontip," Mother Rabbit said. "Now stop worrying; everything will be just fine."

The birds sang their cheerful song and all the townsfolk clapped and smiled. Then Mayor Owl gave a welcome speech.

Mayor Owl cut some colorful paper streamers with his scissors. A hundred red, yellow, and green balloons floated high up, up, up, into the clear, breezy air. Everyone stood up again, whistling and yelling gleefully. The fair was officially open.

The runners jumped around playfully at the starting line. Cottontip was shaking; he was very nervous. Then suddenly, the announcer's voice boomed: "On your mark, get set, GO! The red-and-white checkered flag went down, and the racers darted off like a flash! Down the hill they ran. The crowd clapped. Cottontip's feet were light as air. Chucky Chipmunk and Randolph Rat did their best. Cottontip glided past them. He caught up with Gerry Gerbil and his own cousin, Fuzzy Rabbit. The race was close! Cottontip, Gerry, and Fuzzy, all dashed over the wooden bridge, and down Old Saw Mill Road together. Up the ridge they came and down Main Street they flew!

When Cottontip saw Mrs. Mole at the pie booth, he remembered taking them to her house the day before. Suddenly, VROOM! Cottontip lunged forward and left Gerry and Fuzzy in a cloud of gray dust. On through the final stretch of the race he sped! The crowd's roars and screams were deafening. Mother Rabbit held her paws together and bit her lip. Mrs. Mole stopped selling pies and came from behind her booth to see why everyone was hysterical.

Cottontip broke the red tape as he threw his arms up and leaped over the finish line.

Everybody ran over to see Conttontip's first place medal. It was gold with bright yellow ribbon around the edges. All the friends of Green Patch Cove gathered around him. "Congratulations, Cottontip!" cried Fuzzy Rabbit.

"Yeah, you were great! Gerry Gerbil said, all out of breath. All the friends were amazed and wanted to know how Cottontip had won. Lily asked, "How did you do it? You didn't even practice yesterday."

"Oh yes he did!" beamed Mother
Rabbit.

"He had a carrot-pie practice!"
Cottontip looked at his mother
and they both laughed.

Printed in the United States
By Bookmasters